Always My Brother

Jean Reagan

Illustrated by Phyllis Pollema-Cahill

TILBURY HOUSE, PUBLISHERS · GARDINER, MAINE

My brother John and I were best buddies.

   We were silly together—like when we'd run around barefoot in the snow. And we were serious together—like when we stayed up all night with our dog Toby after he was hit by a car.

   But more than anything else, we loved to play soccer together. As soon as the snow melted every spring, we used to grab the ball and race to the park. John was a goalie. So I shot and he tried to stop 'em. Toby would chase the ball, barking, "Mine, mine, mine!"

   Then John and I would walk home—not touching, but with our shadows holding hands.

John never minded losing a game. I did. When my team lost, I'd glare out the window on the ride home. But even when I wanted to stay grumpy, John could make me laugh.

He'd tap my shoulder and say, "Becky? Knock-knock."

"Who's there?"

"Boo."

"Boo-who?"

"Don't cry. It's just a soccer game."

Once, after my team had a bad loss, John didn't try to make me laugh. Instead, he said, "You should be goalie. You're quick— you could've stopped those goals."

"If we were both goalies, we couldn't practice together," I said.

John nodded. "You're right."

But that was all before—before John died.

Right away, our house filled with family and friends.

Some stayed for days.

When they left, life went back to normal. Only it wasn't normal at all.

At meals I stared at John's empty chair. When we had his favorite—pizza with pineapple—I felt so sad, I ran from the table. And slammed my door. Hard.

In the car I kept looking at John's side. No more knock-knock jokes.

I stopped playing soccer. It wasn't fun anymore.

Without John, our family seemed like a three-legged dog. But not like Toby. Not happy.

On my first day back at school, my friends looked away.
I guess they didn't know what to say. I didn't either.

One night I said, "I just want everyone to act the same as before."

Dad stared out the window. "So do I."

Mom smiled, with tears in her eyes. "It'll get easier—I hope."

Only Toby acted the same. Every time he saw me, he wagged his tail and gave me kisses.

"Toby, don't you care that John's gone?" I asked. Toby kissed me more!

By the time winter came again, I didn't feel so sad when I saw pictures of John. I even smiled when I looked at the one of us in the tub. We were little kids then, with soap-bubble beards and spiky hair. Toby was just a fluff-ball puppy.

One morning, watching Toby roll in the snow,
I actually laughed out loud.

At a friend's party, I
        sang "Happy Birthday" (opera style),
        ate two pieces of cake (with double ice cream), and
        told my favorite knock-knock joke.

When I got home I described the whole party to Mom.
But later I said, "I forgot to miss John."

Mom hugged me and was quiet. Then she asked,
"Remember how John could always make you laugh?"

I nodded.

"Don't you think he'd want you to laugh, even now?"

I looked up at her.

She said softly, "Becky, he'll always be your brother."

I hugged her tighter.

The snow melted—and it was soccer season again. I stared at my ball and then kicked it into the corner. Toby hopped up, chasing it around the room.

Dad said, "Hey, want to practice shooting?"

"No." I looked away and shook my head. "I just can't—"

Dad gave me a squeeze. "I know I'm not the best goalie, but I'll try."

Silly Toby nosed the ball behind the chair and got it stuck.
He whined his "please-oh-please" bark.

Dad and I couldn't help but laugh. I reached for the ball
and said, "Okay, let's go to the park."

Toby sped ahead.

Dad definitely wasn't the best goalie. He didn't crouch like John, dive like John, or leap like John. After a while I said, "Dad, let me try. You shoot."

I crouched, dived, and leaped—exactly like John—and stopped every shot! I smiled to myself. "I am a good goalie!"

At dinner I said, "I've decided to be a goalie."

Dad smiled. "Your team sure could use a good one."

Mom laughed. "No kidding!"

Heading to my first game, I thought about John. I reached out my hand. I showed Mom and Dad how to walk—not touching, but with our shadows holding hands.

TILBURY HOUSE, PUBLISHERS
103 Brunswick Avenue, Gardiner, ME 04345
800–582–1899 · www.tilburyhouse.com

First hardcover edition: June 2009 · 10 9 8 7 6 5 4 3 2 1

To John Reagan Philips (August 2, 1986, to November 3, 2005) and Jane Reagan Philips. Always.

Special thanks for insights and encouragement to Barb Babson, Anne Bowen, Laura Cover, Kristin Dobbin, Sue Gorey, Chris Graham, Becky Hall, Patricia Hermes, Lora Koehler, Sandra McIntyre, Lin Oliver, Bobbie Pyron, Marilyn Quinn, Stephanie Steele (Sharing Place), and, of course, John M. Reagan and Peter Philips. Also, in memory of Rose Deisley, Hillary Dobbin, and Thomas Andrew Maynard.

Library of Congress Cataloging-in-Publication Data

Reagan, Jean, 1965-
   Always my brother / Jean Reagan ; illustrated by Phyllis
Pollema-Cahill. — 1st hardcover ed.
      p. cm.
   Summary: Becky slowly returns to the activities she enjoyed with her
big brother, John, after learning that he is still part of her family,
even after his death.
   ISBN 978-0-88448-313-7 (hardcover : alk. paper)
   [1. Brothers and sisters—Fiction. 2. Death—Fiction. 3.
Grief—Fiction.] I. Pollema-Cahill, Phyllis, ill. II. Title.
   PZ7.R2354Alw 2009
   [E]—dc22   2008045821

Designed by Geraldine Millham, Westport, Massachusetts
Printed and bound by Sung In Printing, South Korea